TONY BR

PLAGUE

OUTBREAK IN LONDON, 1665–1666

■SCHOLASTIC

JOSIAH'S HOUSE

DANIEL'S HOUSE

CHEAPSIDE

ST PAULS

L O

DANIEL'S AUNT
& UNCLE'S HOUSE

SAMUEL'S
HOUSE

ALDGATE

LEADENHALL ST

TOWER OF LONDON

O N

CHAPTER

1

It was late in the evening and I was about to say goodbye to my mother for the very last time. The moment had come for me to try and escape, and I knew that once I left our house I would probably never see her again – not in this life, anyway.

"Are you sure you have everything you need, Daniel?" she whispered. "We should try to fit a warm undershirt into your satchel and some more food."

We were standing in my father's workshop on the ground floor of our house. Mother was holding a candle, its tiny yellow flame pushing the shadows into the corners, the light glinting off the tools scattered on the floor where Father had dropped them. She was wearing a white nightgown and her face was deathly pale, with dark smudges under her eyes. Her black hair hung loose to her shoulders, but I could still see the bruised, painful swellings on both sides of her neck.

I knew she felt really ill and that she was only keeping herself going for my sake. She had spent the previous hour – our final precious moments together – packing my satchel and giving me advice. I stood there in my best jacket and breeches, wearing the stockings she had knitted for me and the shoes she had often polished. I clutched the satchel, feeling as if the world was coming to an end.

"Please, Mother, don't make me do this," I said. I was whispering too and my voice trembled. A tear slid down my cheek. "Let me stay here with you."

I stepped forwards to throw my arms round her, but she quickly backed away. She held up her hands to stop me touching her. "You know that can't be, Daniel," she said. "It's a miracle that you haven't already fallen ill. I hate making you leave, but as God is my witness, I won't let you stay, however much you plead. Your only chance is to escape tonight, before the sickness takes you, as it took your father and brothers."

I had already said goodbye to them. My brothers and father had already been taken by the plague. Father had been the first to fall ill, collapsing in his workshop three days ago. Although it felt like a hundred years of grief and sorrow had passed since then.

"But it's not right," I said. "I would rather stay here and die than leave you!"

"Hush now," she said, her voice gentle. "I'll be with you forever, wherever you are. All you have to do is listen to your heart and you will hear my voice."

I tried arguing with her. I fell to my knees and begged her to let me stay, but she refused to listen, even though she was crying too, the tears dripping off her cheeks. She would not change her mind. Father had often said, "By heaven, Meg, you can be so stubborn!" He had always said it with a loving smile, though. We had been a happy family.

When I was young, life had been tough under the rule of the Puritans, but in 1660 we'd got a new king, King Charles II. The next few years were good – for the country, for London and for my family. Lots of new houses were built, and as Father was a good carpenter, his business had prospered. The Puritans had banned bright clothes, but now everyone wanted them, and Mother was a fine seamstress, so she was soon earning us extra money. My brothers worked with Father, but Mother wanted me to learn to read and write. She sent me to a school in Milk Street, where I did well. Before long, I was reading and writing letters for Father – I loved helping him.

I also loved living in London – it was a wonderful place at that time. I roamed all over the city, from the great houses of the rich on the Strand by the river Thames to the hovels of St Giles beyond the northern wall, and from old St Paul's cathedral on Ludgate Hill in the West to the forbidding castle battlements of the Tower of London in the East. The streets were always busy, full of noise and colour, people buying and selling, talking and arguing. Father told me London was the biggest city in the country by far, with more people in it than pebbles on the banks of the Thames.

Then things started to go wrong. We began hearing rumours about people dying from the plague. It didn't bother us to begin with. The plague had first struck hundreds of years ago, when it was called the Black Death, and it had never really gone away. Every year there were a few plague deaths in the hovels of St Giles to the north-west of the city, but that was where it usually stayed.

Then the number of dead started to rise, as everyone could see in the Bills of Mortality the Lord Mayor ordered to be pasted up everywhere. Last winter, in the early part of 1665, when the weather was cold, the deaths were still in single figures and still mostly confined to St Giles. By the spring, however, it was fifty a week in some parishes and by the summer it was hundreds. It was worst in the poor parts of the city, but no one was truly safe. The rich died too, as did the middling sort of people – like my family.

Many people fled the city and for a while the streets were choked with coaches and carts, with columns of frightened people trudging along beside them. The king left the great Palace of Whitehall with his family and went up the Thames to his other fine home at Hampton Court. But lots of families, including my own, had nowhere to go outside London. Father also said we couldn't abandon our home and leave it unguarded. Thieves would break in as soon as they saw we were gone and they would steal everything we owned.

So we stayed and tried to carry on as before, although that wasn't really possible. Men went round the streets with carts – people called them the dead carts – yelling, "Bring out your dead!" and collecting the bodies of all those who had passed away. London is a city full of churches and their bells rang constantly for the endless funerals. Before long there was no space left in the cemeteries, so the Lord Mayor ordered that enormous pits should be dug for the bodies, both inside the city and beyond the walls.

Some people thought the plague, known as the pestilence, was spread by stray cats, so the Lord Mayor ordered all cats to be killed. But the cats had kept the rats under control and soon there were rats everywhere. The taverns were packed with people trying to have fun in the short time they might have left or making sure they got so drunk they didn't think about death. The churches were also packed with people praying to God to save them and their families.

The plague finally reached our street, Bear Alley, in early June. Within a week most of the doors bore red crosses. When one appeared on the house next to ours, we spent the whole night on our knees praying. I wasn't sure how much good our prayers would do. I didn't say that, of course. How could I, when Father prayed every morning in a loud voice and read us passages from the Bible to give us strength? His favourite was Psalm 23, the one that includes the lines: *Yea, though I walk through the valley of the shadow of death, I will fear no evil: for thou art with me; thy rod and thy staff they comfort me.*

Both my parents had always been strong in their faith. I couldn't let them know that I was confused and wondering if God even cared. As I stood there with my mother on that last night, I knew that her faith in God was all she had left. . .

Suddenly, we heard a familiar loud *BONG!*

sounding over the streets outside. It echoed off the houses and was swiftly followed by another and another. The great bells of old St Paul's Cathedral were being rung to let the city know that it was midnight. Mother and I froze and stared at each other. Then she stepped past me and opened the small window in the workshop's far wall.

"We must hurry!" she hissed, fear and panic in her face. "I hadn't realized it was so late. We're running out of time … the watchman will be back soon!"

CHAPTER

The watchman was supposed to make sure we didn't try to leave. If you were found to have the signs of the sickness – a fever, a cough, painful swellings in your neck or groin or under your arms – you were locked into your house and forbidden to come out. Then a red cross was painted on your front door, along with the words *Lord Have Mercy Upon Us*, and a watchman posted to stand guard. It had happened to us almost immediately after Father had fallen ill. A neighbour had heard Mother's cries when he had collapsed and had reported us to the watch.

Locking plague victims in their homes must have seemed like a good idea to the Lord Mayor and his Aldermen, the people who ran London and made rules in the king's name. They hoped to stop the disease spreading by keeping the sick locked in until they died. But Mother had said it was a bad idea and a death sentence for many. Healthy members of the family and any strangers who were unlucky enough to be visiting at the time were locked in as well, just in case they were already infected but not showing any of the signs yet.

Most of the watchmen were hard men who only cared about money. The Lord Mayor paid them a good wage to keep those who were infected locked in their homes. Our own watchman was a well-known villain in the streets around St Paul's. His name was Bad Barnaby and he had a reputation for violence. People said he would cheerfully cut your throat for a farthing – and he was getting paid a lot more than that to make sure none of us escaped. He was a big, strong man with a shaved head, and he kept a cudgel and a knife tucked into his belt. During the day he would swagger up and down outside our house or stand glowering at the windows with his arms crossed. But I kept an eye on him, and I noticed that late in the evening he would sneak off to The Bear, the rough tavern that gave our alley its name. He would stay there for a few hours, drinking with the other watchmen and assorted ruffians, rogues and villains, usually until after midnight. I told Mother about his nightly disappearances, and she had come up with a plan for my escape. She said I had to climb out of a window and go to my aunt and uncle's house.

BONG! The bells of old St Paul's rang again. *BONG! BONG! BONG!*

"Quickly, Daniel," said Mother. "You need to leave now, before it's too late!"

Perhaps it was the urgency in her voice that pushed me into action, or maybe I was just the kind of son who always did as his mother told him. At least that's what my brothers used to tease me about – as the youngest, they said I was bound to be Mother's favourite. I stepped up to the window, threw my satchel into the alley and started to climb through. It was a tight squeeze and I ended up half falling out, tumbling awkwardly down onto the cobbles. A couple of startled rats ran off down the alley squeaking and squealing.

I jumped to my feet as the last *BONG!* boomed from the cathedral and the bells fell silent. The houses in our alley leaned towards each other, so only a narrow strip of sky was visible. The half-moon lay an eerie silver strip of light along the cobbles, making the shadows on either side deeper and darker. I picked up my satchel and slung it over my shoulder, then turned back to say goodbye to Mother. I opened my mouth, but no words came out. What *do* you say to your mother for the last time in this world, knowing that she is dying? Her face was framed in the window and I could see she was struggling to find the right words too. Her eyes locked onto mine, and we reached out to each other, but our fingertips didn't meet. The sound of footsteps accompanied by loud voices and drunken laughter made us both jump. The watchman was returning, and it sounded as if he wasn't alone.

"Go, Daniel," Mother said. "Remember us to your aunt and uncle. And whatever happens, keep your trust in the Lord our God."

I stared at her, trying to burn her face into my memory forever. I began to sob as I quickly walked away. I tried to stay in the shadows, keeping low and creeping along beside the walls of the other houses as quietly as I could.

"Hey, you!" somebody yelled. "What do you think you're up to? Get back inside with the rest of your family or *I'll* kill you, never mind the plague!"

I looked over my shoulder and saw that it was Bad Barnaby who had called out. He was striding towards me and there were two other men with him, all three of them holding their cudgels and glaring at me, their mean, ugly faces twisted with anger. I began to run. Bad Barnaby cursed loudly.

"God's blood!" he yelled. "After him! Don't let the little swine get away."

I flew down the alley as fast as I could. They chased me, whistling and shouting, their boots crashing on the cobbles, the sound echoing off the walls. At the end of the alley I turned sharply into Bread Street, which was only a little wider, and put on a spurt of speed. Ahead of me was Cheapside, the great road that ran from the east of the city towards old St Paul's.

If I could make it to the cathedral, I might be able to hide there from Bad Barnaby and his companions. But they were still behind me – and they were getting closer. I hated the idea of being caught by them. I didn't want my mother's last efforts to be for nothing.

I ran even faster down the darkened streets of the City of Death, through twisting alleys and narrow streets until, finally, I was running for my life along Cheapside, heading for the vast bulk of the old cathedral at the far end of the street. Its central tower loomed over the buildings around it and I could see a huge procession of people holding lanterns moving towards its doors. A great murmuring rose from them, everyone praying and crying. I had never seen so many people gathered there at night.

I plunged into the crowd and pushed through the packed mass of bodies. I only looked round once I reached the steps leading up to the doors. Bad Barnaby and his companions had stopped in the street – they seemed to have given up the chase. They turned away after a moment, heading back down Cheapside towards Bear Alley. I breathed a sigh of relief and entered the cathedral, leaning against the cool stone wall to catch my breath and wondering how my life had come to this.

The plague wasn't the first terrible thing to happen in London. Just before I was born, civil wars had torn our country apart. King Charles I had fought Parliament for control of the country. The king had said Parliament was trying to take the power given to him by God and Parliament had said he was a tyrant who wanted to steal their freedom. There had been many terrible battles and in the end the king had lost his kingdom – and his head as well. Then England had no king, but a Lord Protector instead, a hard man called Oliver Cromwell, who was a ruthless ruler.

My parents had lived through those times and had often talked about them, so I knew the other reasons behind the troubles. A big one had been religion. England had been a Protestant nation since King Henry VIII broke away from the Catholic Church in order to divorce his wife. But many who opposed King Charles were Puritans, Protestants of an extreme kind. My father hated them and said they were cold-blooded fanatics who didn't like anybody having fun. At any rate, all the theatres had been kept closed for most of the time Cromwell was in charge.

Eventually Cromwell died, but it had been clear for years things had to change.

People were unhappy and the country wasn't being run well. It was decided that we should have a king again and the son of the dead king was invited to rule over us. His name was also Charles and he had been living as an exile in France for years. He returned – as King Charles II – in the year of our Lord 1660. It was known as the Restoration of the monarchy, a great change in our history.

I was seven that year, but I remember how joyful people were. There were parties and processions and the theatres soon reopened. It seemed that a new age had begun, one in which we would be allowed to enjoy ourselves again. The new king was tall and handsome and always well dressed. To begin with he was very popular, although there were still plenty of sour-faced Puritans who thought we shouldn't have a king. But for the most part they kept their own counsel. Then the plague had come and the king had fled, leaving us Londoners to our fate.

CHAPTER

3

I had been inside St Paul's many times before. It was the heart of London. Religious services were held there every day, but people also visited the cathedral to hear the latest news and gossip, and to be seen in their fashionable clothes. Normally, the middle aisle – which everybody called Paul's Walk – was entirely given over to these crowds. Day and night, the buzz of lively conversation rose into the great open space beneath the high roof.

Tonight it couldn't have felt more different.

The cathedral was filled with shadows, and the light of candles and lanterns was lost in the darkness. It was packed and I was surprised that nobody seemed worried about being so close to other people. I saw many with the signs of the sickness, people who were clearly feverish, their necks swollen. Most of them were being cared for by family and friends. I wondered if they had escaped from their locked houses, just like me. The noise was deafening – terrible cries and shouts, people wailing and praying in front of the great altar, preachers calling out, "Repent! Repent!"

Suddenly, I realized how tired I was. I had barely slept for the last three nights and running from Bad Barnaby had worn me out. I was supposed to be on my way to the house of Aunt Mary, my mother's sister, and her husband, Uncle John. Mother was sure they would be free of the plague as they lived outside the eastern wall, beyond Aldgate. But their house was a long way from St Paul's and I needed to rest. I also wanted to avoid running into Bad Barnaby again.

I decided to spend the night in the cathedral. It had many nooks and crannies, odd corners in the side chapels where I could hide and get some peace.

It took me a while, but I found the perfect spot – a small space behind the tomb of some knight who had long been forgotten. I curled up on the cold stone floor with my head resting on my satchel and tried to sleep. It was hard with all the noise, but eventually I must have drifted off.

I woke with a start and thought I was still in my own bed at home. I had dreamed of the happy times I had shared with my family. For a moment I expected to hear their voices, my father and brothers laughing downstairs, Mother calling for me to come and eat my breakfast before they did. Then I heard a cry of despair and a voice praying, and I remembered what had happened and where I was. Hot tears filled my eyes and I sat hugging my knees.

I knew I couldn't sit like that forever, though. Mother wanted me to survive and I had to try. I wiped the tears from my face and pulled myself together. Mother had put some bread and cheese in my satchel and a flask containing some small beer. I ate and drank, and forced myself to think about the journey ahead of me rather than what had happened, or whether Mother was still alive. I took a deep breath and left my hiding place.

The cathedral was just as packed as last night but much quieter, with many people sleeping. Pale light seeped in through the great stained-glass windows, spreading colours over the bodies in the pews. It was still very early in the morning. *All the better for me*, I thought. Villains like Bad Barnaby were creatures of the night – I had noticed that he often dozed in the early hours of the day. Even so, before I left the cathedral I still peeked round one of the great doors to make sure he wasn't waiting.

I headed east, back down Cheapside towards Aldgate, leaving St Paul's behind me. The sun was warm, the sky blue and cloudless. On such a lovely morning last summer the streets would already have been full of people cheerfully going about their business. But everywhere was eerily quiet, the shops and houses shut and locked. I saw many doors with red crosses painted on them and the few people I spotted scuttled away, keeping their distance.

This part of the city had been struck hardest by the pestilence – St Giles was just beyond the city wall to the north-west. The streets gradually seemed more normal as I walked eastwards, people coming and going, a few shops and taverns open, a rich man on a fine white horse clip-clopping down the middle of the road as if he owned it. But there were still plenty of red crosses. The people here seemed just as scared and there were ranting preachers on almost every corner.

The Puritan preachers said the plague was God's punishment for bringing back the king and "turning away from the Path of the Righteous", and many people thought they were right. I remember one man in particular. He had preached on the corner of Bread Street every day for years, ranting and raving and telling everyone that they were sinners and doomed. People had ignored him, but once the plague really got going he was always surrounded by a crowd. They stood and listened, hands clasped in prayer and fear in their eyes.

"Repent!" the preacher said. "This city has fallen under the dark wing of God's Destroying Angel!"

The crowd had looked up, terrified, even though the sun shone in a clear blue sky.

It was the middle of the morning by the time I reached Aldgate. I walked through the ancient archway, following a wagon pulled by two big horses, the driver hunched over the reins, the wheels rumbling over the cobbles. Two women sat in the back, one old and the other young. A boy of about five sat by them and the young woman was crying, tears rolling down her cheeks onto a baby in her arms. I looked away, sure that if I watched her for too long I would start crying as well. I had seen many unhappy and grieving people that morning, but something about this young mother upset me more than all the others. I couldn't work it out at first, but then I realized she reminded me of my own mother, who I would never see again.

Aunt Mary and Uncle John lived on a street a few minutes' walk beyond Aldgate, near the Angel Inn. They didn't have any children, but they were happy, hard-working and decent people. Mary was a seamstress like Mother and John was a cooper, making barrels for anyone who would pay. We had seen them quite often before the plague came and I knew that they would take me in without question.

I turned the corner of their street at last – and stopped in my tracks. A red cross had been roughly daubed on their door and the paint had run down the planks in lines, like blood from a wound. Beneath the cross were the usual words, *Lord Have Mercy Upon Us*. But the door was half open, the wood around the lock smashed and splintered. My stomach tightened with fear and suddenly I felt sick. Had my uncle and aunt been struck down by the plague as well?

I don't know how long I stood there staring at the door. I was shivering, even though the day was quite hot now, the sun's rays beating down on my head. I didn't want to go into the house, but I made myself do it. The rooms were empty, my aunt and uncle's bed strewn with dirty sheets, the cupboards open and anything valuable taken. I was confused, wondering what had happened. I tried not to think the worst. Eventually, I stumbled outside to ask one of their neighbours.

It took me a long time to find anyone. Most of the other doors in the street had red crosses on them and those that didn't stayed firmly shut however hard I knocked. At last an old woman opened an upstairs window and asked me what I wanted.

"Do you know what's happened to my Aunt Mary and Uncle John?" I said. "They live just along the street, but they're not in their house and all their things are missing."

"Are you stupid, boy?" snapped the old woman. "They're dead and gone, like almost everyone in this street. The dead cart men smashed their door in yesterday and took them off to a plague pit. They probably took everything else they could lay their hands on as well, but that's what men like them do these days..."

I couldn't stand to hear any more and walked away. Grief for my poor aunt and uncle filled my heart. But I felt anxious for myself as well. Mother had been so sure they would be able to take me in that we hadn't talked about what to do if the plan failed. We had no other family and there was no one else I could turn to for help. Mother had given me some money, but it was only a few shillings and I knew it wouldn't last long. I briefly thought that I should flee from London and go into the country. But what would be the point? I was a London boy, born and bred. I had never left the city in my life, not even once. Besides, we had already heard that people in the country villages chased away anyone from London in case they brought the plague with them.

So I wiped the tears from my cheeks again and headed back towards Aldgate. I had decided to go back to St Paul's, thinking that I might find food and something to drink there. I had eaten all the bread and cheese in my satchel, and I was beginning to feel hungry.

I trudged westwards through the city along Cheapside and reached the cathedral by early afternoon. But it was even more crowded than before, and suddenly I didn't want to be in a place with so many people. I couldn't face the noise and the sadness and the fear – all those desperate families in search of salvation, or even just some hope. All it did was make me think of my own family.

I'm not sure what I did after that. I remember walking away from the cathedral, heading north towards Cripplegate, but my head was aching and my stomach hurt, and I wondered if the plague had finally caught up with me. The afternoon grew hotter and I began to feel dizzy as I wandered the streets.

I could hear church bells ringing and people calling out. After a while I found myself alone in a courtyard and I sat down to rest.

I must have fallen asleep. When I woke up the sun was setting and shadows were filling the courtyard. On one side there was a blacksmith's with a stable beside it. Beyond that a narrow alley led to some houses. Suddenly, a figure appeared in the alley and moved towards me. My blood ran cold. The figure was like a creature from a nightmare – from the neck down it looked like a man dressed in black, but its head was like a bird's with a giant beak.

I stared in horror, convinced that Death himself had come to collect me.

CHAPTER

The figure loomed over me and I closed my eyes, sure I was doomed. Part of me welcomed the idea of dying and going to Heaven. At least there I might see my family again, and I wouldn't have to keep worrying about what to do next, either. But another part of me desperately wanted to survive.

Nothing happened and after a while I dared to open my eyes. The figure was bending down to examine me and I could see now that it wore a black hat with a broad rim and that the beak was brown and leathery. Above it was a pair of watery brown eyes that looked strangely like those of an ordinary man. I could hear the figure's breathing, a sound that somehow seemed too loud.

Then the figure did something I wasn't expecting – it took off its hat and beak, revealing an ordinary man beneath them. He had black hair, a beard with grey streaks and a big fleshy nose that I could see was red even in the gloom. He stared at me intensely, looking me up and down like a man studying a horse or a dog he was thinking of buying. At last he nodded and held out his hand.

"Come with me, boy," he said in a deep voice. "If you want to live, that is."

I was exhausted and had no other option, so I took his hand and went with him into the night. I followed the man through the dark streets to his house. It lay in a narrow alley off Blowbladder Street, between Cheapside and Newgate. Like him, the house was tall and thin, each room lit by candles and filled with strange objects – shelves packed with bottles of brightly coloured powders or liquids, or dead creatures such as snakes and lizards and bats, many with their innards showing. There were also jars with body parts in them – hearts and livers, lungs and tongues. To begin with I thought they were from animals too, but then I wondered if they might have been taken from people.

Other shelves were filled with books. At home we only had a few books – our family Bible and the prayer books we used in church. But this man must have had more than fifty, some with richly decorated spines and covers, many that looked very old. Several lay open on a table in the middle of the largest room. There were lots of glass jars and vials on the table too, and a stone pestle and mortar.

The man pulled out a chair for me at the table. He cleared some space, pushing aside the books and the jars and vials, and put a bowl of soup and some bread in front of me. At first I held back, scared that the lumps of meat I saw in the soup might have come from one of those jars on the shelves. But the soup smelled good and my stomach was rumbling, so before long I was eagerly filling my belly.

"Ah, is it not a good thing to satisfy those who are hungry?" said the man, with a big smile. "Whoever comes to me will never be in want – or die of the pestilence. For I am sent by the Lord to bring help to all those in need – including you, boy."

"Are you a priest?" I asked. He seemed a funny sort of priest to me, but I couldn't think who else would say the Lord had sent them.

"I am a plague doctor," the man said. "You may call me Doctor Beak."

I had heard of plague doctors, but I had never come across one until now. I had some idea they cared for the sick and made medicines to fight the plague, but I didn't know much more. Now I discovered that was only the half of it. Doctor Beak seemed to like the sound of his own voice, so I said nothing and just listened as he talked to me about his work. He told me that he taught people how to avoid the plague and had even written pamphlets on the subject. He also made herbal plasters to put on the swellings, which he called buboes, as well as various potions to drink.

"But why do you wear that strange mask?" I said when I'd finished the soup.

"To protect me from the miasma of course, the foul vapour that fills the houses of the sick," he said, as if it was obvious. "We cannot see the miasma, but believe me, it is the thing that has brought the sickness, a deadly poison that seeps upwards from the ground beneath the worst parts of the city. The beak part of the mask is filled with marjoram and thyme and rosemary, herbs that keep the miasma out."

He told me that all the plague doctors wore these masks and so people had come to call them all Doctor Beak, almost as if there was only one of them, who appeared as if by magic in every part of the city. There was certainly an air of sorcery about the costume and the mask and the house. It made me uneasy. I had heard many sermons in church about the terrible evil of sorcery and how it was an abomination before God.

But my own Doctor Beak had given me soup and bread, and didn't seem like a sorcerer. He was even happy to tell me his real name, which was Josiah Hopkins. Besides, most of the priests and vicars who had given those sermons had long since fled the city, while Josiah had stayed to help the people. As far as I could see, that made him a good man.

"I believe it was God's will that brought us together,

Daniel," he said. "I need an assistant, someone to help me in my work of curing the suffering. Will you agree to join me on my mission to save the sick?"

I didn't know if God's will had brought us together or not, but his talk of cures for sickness had filled my heart with hope. Besides, I wanted to do something to fight the plague.

"I would be happy to be your assistant," I said. "But I have one request. I want you to visit my house and help my mother."

If Mother was still alive – and there was a chance she was – then perhaps Doctor Beak might be able to save her with one of his potions or remedies.

"Why, of course!" said Josiah, beaming. "Tell me exactly what I will find there."

I told him about my family and how the plague had carried off my father and brothers, and how I had escaped. He stopped smiling and frowned instead as he listened. For a brief instant I worried that he might chase me from his house or even hand me over to the watchmen. After all, had I not broken the Lord Mayor's rule? But then he smiled again and patted me on the shoulder.

"You have walked through the valley of the shadow of death," he said. "But you are still a good son who wishes to save his mother. I will grant your request."

"Thank you!" I said. I fell to my knees in front of him and kissed his hand, as I had seen people kiss the hands of priests. "Please, can we go now?"

"Alas, I do not think such a course of action would be wise," he said. "The streets are full of all sorts of rogues at this time of night. No, we will go tomorrow."

I tried to get him to change his mind, but he was just as stubborn as Mother. I knew he was probably right, too. Certain areas of the city had always been dangerous at night, and if Bad Barnaby and his friends were anything to go by, the pestilence had made the streets even worse. So at last I gave up and tried to be patient.

Josiah showed me where I was to spend the night – a small box bed in the corner of the scullery. He went off to his own room and I lay down, but sleep wouldn't come. I had suddenly realized that I might run into Bad Barnaby again when I took Josiah to my house. Would he try and seize me? I shuddered. I didn't like that idea at all – but then what did it matter? It would be a small price to pay if it meant saving Mother's life. And with that thought in my head I fell asleep.

The next morning I could hardly wait to set off, but Josiah was very slow to rise and take his breakfast of bread and several glasses of wine. He also went on about my new "duties" – I had to carry a large wooden box full of potions and other things. It had a leather strap to go over my shoulder and it was quite heavy. I didn't care about that, though. I just wanted to get going.

Eventually we left, and I hurried through the streets, ignoring the few people who were about. I checked every so often that Josiah – or Doctor Beak as I had to call him when he was wearing his plague doctor outfit – was keeping up with me. Bear Alley wasn't far from Blowbladder Street and we soon arrived. I turned the corner and looked out for Bad Barnaby, but there was no one in the alley at all.

I quickly walked up to my house and stood in front of it. My blood went cold. The door was half open and the wood around the lock was smashed and splintered, just as it had been at my aunt and uncle's. I dropped the box and ran inside, calling, "Mother!" over and over again, my voice echoing in the empty rooms. But I had realized why there was no watchman to guard the house and I knew there would be no reply.

I was too late.

CHAPTER

5

I flung myself onto my parents' bed, buried my face in the sheets that still smelled of them and sobbed. If I had felt alone when I had discovered my aunt and uncle were dead, at that moment I felt doubly so. Although Mother had been under the shadow of death when I had last seen her, deep down I suppose I had refused to believe that she would actually die. Meeting Josiah had filled me with hope, too. But now Mother was truly gone.

Eventually, I ran out of tears and sat up. My heart

was broken and I was full of grief. Yet I didn't want to give in. I owed it to Mother to survive, to stay alive and somehow keep the family going. Who would remember them if I died now? We would be like the dust in the streets that is blown away by the wind.

I took a deep breath, got up from the bed and went downstairs in search of Josiah. I found him in the parlour, standing by the table where we had always eaten our family meals. The room had been thoroughly ransacked, the cupboards emptied of Mother's linen and the cutlery, the chairs knocked over and broken. But something of ours had been left – Josiah was holding our Bible.

"May I offer you my humble condolences, Daniel?" he said, his voice full of sympathy. "I can hardly imagine your pain and suffering at this time of sorrow. If only I had visited your house before... I fear this holy book is all that remains of your family's earthly goods." He laid a hand on my shoulder and smiled. "But what more does a soul need in this vale of tears than the word of the Lord our God?"

He handed me the Bible and I looked inside the

cover, where Mother had asked me to write down our names and our dates of birth. Josiah's words were an echo of the last words I had heard Mother say and I took that as a good omen. Perhaps she was watching me from Heaven, pleased that I had someone to look out for me and that I was helping him perform a worthy task. That felt like a very good thought and I held on to it.

"Well, time to move on," said Josiah. "There's no peace for the wicked."

I almost smiled. Father had often used the same phrase and Mother had always laughed, saying that no one could have been less wicked than him. But I felt my eyes prickling with tears again. Josiah was right, there was nothing in this empty shell of a house any more, just a host of sad memories and the ghosts of our past. So I left with Josiah to discover what life might have in store for me next.

After we left my family's house, we went back to Blowbladder Street to begin work. Once there, Josiah simply walked up and down, waiting for the suffering to approach him. He told me he had no real need to proclaim himself.

"My outer garments do that very well," he said. "Especially the mask."

Around mid-morning, people began coming up to him, seeking medicines for their stricken family or friends. He would talk to them, his voice made strangely muffled by his mask, asking them what tokens of the sickness their loved ones displayed. When they answered he would pause to think for a while, nodding his beaked head, and then turn to me. I would open the box and he would remove whatever potion he deemed suitable.

The first time this happened, I was shocked to hear Josiah ask to be paid. I suppose I had never thought that money would be involved when it came to saving people's lives. The price of the potion was five shillings, which seemed a lot to me – the vial of liquid was quite small. The man who wanted it for his wife was clearly a labourer, his clothes rough and homespun, and five shillings was a lot of money for someone like that, enough to live on for a week. Yet he put the coins in Josiah's hand without hesitation and looked at the potion with wonder. But then Josiah *had* just told him it was made of the tears Jesus himself had cried.

"You know the story, my friend," said Josiah. "Jesus wept when he saw Lazarus lying dead, but then our Lord brought Lazarus back to life. Go now and give your wife this potion to drink so she will be strong enough to fight death..."

A few moments later another man came up to us and asked for medicine. I could tell immediately that he was wealthier than the first man. This one wore a good hat, jacket and breeches, and his shoes were of a decent quality. He had the look of the printers and booksellers you might see in the streets near St Paul's – a man with a stake in life, as my father would have said. But he was as desperate as the first man and wanted a potion to save his two daughters.

"Ah, I have just the thing," said Josiah, handing him a vial of liquid, which looked identical to the one he had given to the first man. "This is the finest *aqua vitae*, distilled by philosophers at Oxford University, and guaranteed to keep the four humours balanced in anyone who drinks it regularly. And all that for just five pounds. You'll take two? Don't stand there gawping, Daniel – serve the gentleman!"

I was gawping because I could hardly believe what

I had just heard. Ten pounds was enough for a family to live on for a whole month! But the man paid up and he dashed off, carefully holding the two little vials as if they were most precious things in all God's creation. I could understand that, though. I was sure Father would have paid all the money he had to save William, Henry, Mother and me. Yet I still felt uneasy and I began to watch Josiah more closely.

Over the next few days, my uneasiness deepened. We visited different parts of the city, selling cures to the rich and poor. Josiah's prices varied wildly, he spoke differently to everyone and he sold a lot more than just potions. There were amulets to wear round the neck, small bags of "magical herbs" and "garlic to ward off evil spirits", and even simple good luck charms like rabbits' feet. It all sounded like nonsense to me or, even worse, sorcery. There were "soothing elixirs" too, and more *aqua vitae* distilled by philosophers at Oxford". Josiah also sold quite a few of his pamphlets to those who could read. No wonder the box I carried for him was so heavy.

Sometimes we were invited into the houses of the sick. It turned out that some watchmen were happy to be bribed by the people they were supposed to be guarding. For the right amount of money they would let visitors into the houses, and I soon found myself wondering if they could be bribed to let families out as well. Perhaps the people with the tokens of the plague I had seen at St Paul's had bought their way out instead of escaping.

To me those visits were like journeys into Hell itself. I will never forget the darkened houses, the foul smells of the sickness, the desperate, anxious families watching over loved ones. Josiah sold them all the things he had in his box – potions and amulets and herbs, as well as herbal plasters for the swellings. In some houses he prayed like a priest, begging God to spare the sinners who were dying. In others he chanted strange rhymes and talked about the influence of the stars.

Each night, long after the sun had set over the city, we would return to his house. Once there I would make supper for us both. After the first night, Josiah had made it clear my duties also included preparing his meals, washing his clothes and cleaning his home. We ate well, as Josiah supplied several shopkeepers with potions and cures in return for food. Supplies in London were growing short, as farmers were reluctant to bring their produce to the city for fear of the plague. People were beginning to go hungry, so I knew I was lucky. But I didn't feel it. One evening, my unhappiness must have shown on my face.

"I see doubt in your eyes, Daniel," Josiah said, pushing his bowl aside and turning to me. "What have I done to offend you?"

My parents had taught me to be honest, so I told him the things that were worrying me.

"How can you charge so much money for your cures?" I asked. "I know you prepare all the potions and remedies yourself. Why do you charge rich people more? And why—"

"Ah, Daniel," he interrupted, shaking his head. "These mysteries are easily solved. A man must make a living and I fix my prices according to what I judge each person can pay. I also talk to them in ways that I think will have most influence on them – some prefer religion, while others like a little magic with their medicine. But it is all for a good cause, is it not? I am doing God's work, if sometimes not in God's way."

It sounded reasonable when he put it like that. Perhaps it didn't matter how he performed his work, so long as it calmed people who were frightened and cured those who were ill. So I decided to keep believing that he was a good man – at least until I had sure proof that he wasn't.

I didn't have to wait long.

CHAPTER

6

One morning a few days later, Josiah announced that we would be going somewhere different to sell his wares. I wasn't surprised. I had noticed there were fewer and fewer people around the streets we usually visited. The plague had done its work all too well in that part of the city, and now that it was July and the height of summer, it was raging more fiercely through the eastern streets and had even jumped across the River Thames to Southwark. The Bills of Mortality were still being pasted up and they showed that thousands of people were dying in the city every week.

We set off, heading towards Bishopsgate. It was a warm, sunny day and there had been no rain for weeks, so the streets were dry and dusty. The box of potions and remedies felt even heavier in the heat, the leather strap biting into my shoulder. I couldn't help thinking that the "cures" didn't seem to have saved many people, judging by the rising number of plague victims. We passed several bodies left lying in the street, even though the dead carts seemed to be everywhere, each one heaped with corpses, rich and poor thrown in together.

Eventually we came to the small square outside St Helen's Church at Bishopsgate, where we found more people. Soon business was quite brisk, although I could tell Josiah was struggling in the heat, sweat running down his neck from beneath his mask. But I realized that without it he would lose the very strangeness that was part of his appeal. I doubted people would be so easily convinced by his cures if he no longer looked like Doctor Beak, just an ordinary man like anyone else. So he kept going, huffing and puffing and getting cross. But he soon got fed up.

"That's enough for one day," he said after only an hour or so. "I am sorely in need of a drink."

He hurried off, ignoring the people who still wanted to buy potions, angrily waving away those who came up to him, and headed for the small tavern in the corner of the square. He ducked through the door, removing his mask as he did so. I made as if to follow him, but he waved me away too, telling me to wait outside. So I found a patch of shade and did as I was told. But after a few minutes I was just too thirsty and decided to risk going into the tavern in search of a cooling drink.

I pushed the door open and went inside. The tavern consisted of a long room with a low ceiling. One side was divided into several booths, each with a table and benches. On the other side stood a bar with a bald, ugly man behind it. To begin with I couldn't see Josiah, but then I heard his voice and that of another man coming from a booth. I couldn't make out what they were saying, but there was something about the tone of their voices that made me suspicious. The man behind the bar was looking the other way, so I slipped into the booth next to Josiah's and listened.

"So you've come to steal my thunder, have you, Josiah?" said the other man. "Well, if that's the case, you can turn right round and go back to Blowbladder Street this instant. There certainly isn't enough business around here for two Doctor Beaks."

"Don't be like that, Isaac. I only came in for a pot of ale. Making a profit from the sick is thirsty work. But you have nothing to fear from me – I am thinking of retiring. I am far too old to be trudging round London in this heat wearing that mask. Some days I can hardly breathe..."

"I know what you mean," said this Isaac. "But it's a small price to pay, isn't it? Why, thanks to the plague, I have more money than I've ever had before. Death has been very kind to me, so I hope the plague keeps going for quite some time."

"I agree, my friend," said Josiah, laughing. "I must also confess it gives me even more pleasure to know that I am taking money from fools. Anyone who is stupid enough to believe they can be cured by one of my potions is probably better off dying from the plague anyway. . ."

As I sat there listening, any faith I still had in Josiah drained away. I saw that he *was* wicked after all, a villain like Bad Barnaby, although of a different kind. Josiah's weapons were the smooth words that flowed from his mouth. He had realized that I came from a godly family, so he had spoken to me like a godly man himself. But that had been all lies and pretence, as was everything about him.

I felt a dark cloud of gloom settle over me. So much for the "worthy task" that would give my life meaning. All I had done was help a rogue give false hope to those who were suffering and dying, just so he could take whatever money they had.

"I tell you what, Josiah," said Isaac, his words penetrating the fog of despair in my brain. "I hear you've got a new boy and that he looks a lot healthier than your last one. If you're really thinking of retiring, I'd be happy to take him off your hands. Shall we say two pounds?"

"What kind of a fool do you take *me* for?" said Josiah. "I've had three boys as my assistants and none of them lasted long. But I have begun to think young Daniel will live forever, such is his resistance to the sickness. Why, you can say he is proof of your remedies. . . For that reason I will not take a penny less than twenty pounds. He will be a sound investment, Isaac, one guaranteed to bring you a profit."

They haggled over my price as if I were a farm animal to be bought and sold at a whim, and I sat there horrified, my mind reeling. Was it true that I had some kind of special resistance to the sickness? I had begun to wonder why so many people around me became ill and died, while I stayed healthy. Then I felt a hot wave of anger. The only thing that mattered now was to tell these two evil men they couldn't do what they wanted with me. I would not be their slave.

I rose from my seat and went round to stand at the end of their booth. Both men fell silent and looked up at me. Isaac was a scrawny man with a hard face and mean eyes that bored into mine. Josiah looked a little surprised, then he frowned.

"I thought I told you to stay outside, Daniel," he said.

"I've been listening to you," I said, spitting the words out. "You won't sell me to this man, nor to anyone else. Goodbye, Josiah, I hope I never see you again." I turned to leave, but Josiah grabbed my wrist and pulled me sharply towards him.

"Not so fast," he muttered. Our eyes met and it was as if a second mask had suddenly fallen from his face, revealing the evil of his true nature. He slowly tightened his grip on my wrist, doing his best to hurt me and make me do what he wanted. Isaac and the man behind the bar looked on, smirking. I lowered my head and bit Josiah's hand, sinking my teeth in. He cursed and pushed me away. I almost fell, but managed to stay on my feet and get to the door. I could taste Josiah's blood in my mouth as I ran across the square. I didn't stop to spit it out for a very long time.

When I finally stopped running, I was back on Cheapside, near the Church of St Mary-le-Bow. I ducked down a narrow alley and found a quiet corner where I could catch my breath and work out what to do next. I was sure Josiah and Isaac would come after me eventually – it seemed I was worth money to them. I would have to watch out for them wherever I went, which would make life difficult. But then it was going to be difficult anyway – I had no home and no means of making a living.

In fact I had nothing except for my satchel and our family's Bible. Both were still under my bed in Josiah's house. I knew it would have been wise to leave them there, but I couldn't do that. I wasn't going to let Josiah keep them. Apart from my clothes, they were the only things that linked me to my family. I reckoned Josiah would stay in the tavern with Isaac for a while longer. I would hopefully have time to do what I needed to.

I ran through the streets under the hot sun and soon arrived at Blowbladder Street, when I realized the flaw in my plan. Josiah worried constantly that thieves might break into his house, so he always made sure his door was locked while he was out, and he kept the only key on a chain round his neck.

How was I going to get inside? I remembered one of the windows at the rear of the house had a loose catch. I crept down the alley beside the house and found the right window. I got my fingertips under the frame and pulled. It took a while, but the catch eventually gave and the window swung open. I climbed up, scrambled inside and made straight for the scullery, where I grabbed my things.

I stuffed the Bible into the satchel, then had a last look round Josiah's house. I felt like smashing his jars and bottles so he couldn't concoct his fake potions any more, but I knew there was no point in that. Even if Josiah didn't make and sell them, there were others who would, villains like Isaac. In any case, I needed to get out of there as quickly as possible – Josiah might return at any moment.

I couldn't go through the front door as it was still locked – I would have to leave the way I'd come in. So once again I found myself throwing my satchel into the street and climbing through a window, as I had the night I had left my family home. This one was just as tight a fit and I fell awkwardly onto the cobbles as before.

Someone stepped out of the shadows on the other side of the street and stood over me, although all I could see of him was a pair of heavy boots.

"God's blood!" said a voice I half recognized. "It's that boy who escaped!"

I slowly raised my eyes and terror filled my heart – it was Bad Barnaby!

Then he hit me with his cudgel and the world went dark.

CHAPTER

When I came round, my hands were tied behind my back and I was being dragged down the street. My legs and feet bumped over the cobbles, Bad Barnaby's boots striding ahead of me. After a while we stopped, a door was opened and I was taken into a small, evil-smelling room and dumped on the floor.

I lay there for a moment trying to pull myself together. Then someone emptied a bucket of cold water on my face and I sat up sharply, coughing and spluttering. I shook my head, wiped my eyes and looked around. Bad Barnaby was looking down on me with a horrible smirk on his face. Behind him were the other two watchmen who had chased me on the night I had escaped from Bear Alley. My heart was thudding and I wondered why they hadn't killed me already.

"Well, this is a strange encounter and no mistake," said Bad Barnaby. "I'd have thought you'd be dead and buried in a plague pit by now. The rest of your family probably ended up that way. But here you are, large as life, breathing like the rest of us. Although I'll wager you've been spreading the pestilence to all and sundry. Not that it needs much help, does it lads? Welcome to Armageddon!"

The three of them laughed, but my attention had been caught by a small part of what Bad Barnaby had said – "your family probably ended up that way". Those few words opened up all sorts of possibilities – perhaps Mother was alive after all!

"Don't you know for sure what happened to my mother, then?" I said. "You were our watchman. I thought you were supposed to stay right until the end, until everyone was dead."

Bad Barnaby stopped laughing and his smile vanished. He bent down to look in my eyes, his nose almost touching mine, his breath foul. I turned my face to the side.

"You put an end to that, you little swine," he hissed, spit from his mouth spraying onto my cheek. "I lost my position that night because you escaped, so I have no idea what happened to your mother. I know what's going to happen to you, though."

"Wh-what do you mean?" I said. I had been shaking with fear, but now I went still. There was no longer a part of me that wanted to die. I badly wanted to live.

"You're going to be our little helper," he said, smiling once more. "I lost a lot of money because of you, so you owe me. I should think you could pay off your debt to me in, oh, a couple of years. So long as you don't catch the plague and die, and you might where you're going. . ."

All three of them laughed, slapping each other on the back as if that was the funniest thing they had ever heard in their lives. I sat on the floor watching them and wondered what new world of madness I had fallen into. They stopped laughing after a while and Bad Barnaby turned to me again.

"Don't look so confused, boy," he said. "It's very simple. There's plenty of loot in houses where everyone has died, but it's hard to tell from the outside which ones they are. You don't want to go blundering in if anyone is still alive. The watchmen and the dead cart men are always at the right place at the right time, so they've been getting into the best houses before me, Ned and George. But now we've got you as our scout and you're good at climbing through windows. . ."

My heart sank – so that was his plan. I couldn't think of anything worse. I had a good idea of what I would find inside the houses because of my visits to the sick with Josiah. Each was more or less the same – eerily quiet, smelling of sickness and fear and death. I had already seen many things that I would never forget and I didn't want to see any more.

"You can't be serious," I said, shaking my head. "I won't do it!"

"Who said you had a choice?" growled Bad Barnaby, slowly drawing his cudgel from his belt. "Do as I say or I'll make you wish you'd never been born."

I held his gaze, tempted to refuse again. But I knew Mother would tell me to do whatever it took to survive. So I held my tongue and looked away.

They made something to eat and then George untied me while Ned searched through my things, soon finding and taking my few shillings. Their clothes were rough and their manners rougher. Ned was tall and thin, with greasy dark hair, while red-haired George was short and very bandy-legged, and they both obeyed Bad Barnaby's every command.

After a night of broken sleep on the floor of their hovel, Bad Barnaby kicked me awake and we set out onto the streets of Farringdon. They took me to an alley where many of the doors bore red crosses. It was deserted and we stopped outside one of the houses.

"Right, in you go, boy," said Bad Barnaby, nodding at a window in front of us. "Just tell us if they're all dead in there and then we'll smash in the door."

The window was small, like most windows in London houses – certainly not big enough for men like Bad Barnaby, Ned and George to climb through. Nothing seemed to be stirring inside. Ned prized the window open with his knife and then I climbed in, steeling myself to whatever horrors I might find. The rooms were dark and filled with familiar smells. There were two bodies in one of the rooms, and I quickly hurried on to the next, shivering. There were no other bodies in the house, at any rate. I climbed back out and told Bad Barnaby.

"That wasn't so bad, was it?" he said, grinning. "Smash the door in, lads!"

I climbed through the windows of four more houses down that alley and only found more of the dead. Afterwards, Bad Barnaby and his companions went out to celebrate their good fortune, leaving me chained up in the hovel. The next day was the same and the day after. Soon it felt as if my life had always been this way. I could barely remember what it had been like before the plague...

August came and the weather grew hotter, the merciless sun beating down every day. I was often on the streets with Bad Barnaby, Ned and George, so I knew that in some parts of the city people still ventured out and tried to go shopping or meet friends as if there were no plague. But many streets were deserted now, except for the dead carts – and men such as Bad Barnaby and his companions. Once in a while I glimpsed a Doctor Beak and found myself wondering if I would have been better off with someone like Josiah, which shows just how low I had sunk.

The worst part of being held captive by Bad Barnaby, Ned and George was having to listen to them. They were so full of themselves, delighted there was no authority any more that could stop them doing whatever they wanted – not the Lord Mayor and his Aldermen, not even the king. But something else gave them even greater satisfaction – the fact that they hadn't caught the plague.

"Do you think it means we're among God's Chosen?" said Ned one evening.

"Only if God's Chosen are the worst rogues in London," said George. "Mind you, I'll bet most of the bishops are still alive, so that proves God loves a villain."

They all roared with laughter and slapped each other on the back again. Their words gave me a lot to think about. Like Josiah and Isaac, they were very bad men, but they were still alive – and I knew that many good people had died, my family among them. I also knew my parents would have said that it was God's will and we could never understand all God's reasons. But it still seemed wrong.

As the weeks went on, however, Bad Barnaby's luck began to run out. Sometimes we arrived at a promising house only to find another gang had beaten us to it. This usually just led to cursing and yelling, but on a couple of occasions fights broke out. The violence didn't usually last long, but I still did my best to stay out of the way.

One morning, Bad Barnaby decided we wouldn't be breaking into houses any more.

"I've got a much better idea," he said. "We're going back to being footpads."

It was a word every Londoner knew well. Footpads were men who robbed people in the street. They hid in the shadows, waiting for victims to walk by, then leaped out and threatened to hurt them unless they handed over their money. I wasn't surprised Bad Barnaby and his companions had been footpads – it was the kind of evil thing they would do. I thought it meant my captivity was over, but I was wrong.

"So you won't be needing me to climb in any more windows," I said.

"Maybe not," said Bad Barnaby. "But I do have another task for you."

My heart sank once more – would all this go on forever?

CHAPTER

There was no time to argue. We left the hovel immediately and headed straight for St Paul's – Bad Barnaby said it would be the best place to find someone to rob. I hadn't been to that part of the city for a while, and when we arrived I noticed there weren't many people around. It was hotter than ever, the sun like a great ball of fire in the clear blue sky.

"Looks like lean pickings for footpads, Barnaby," muttered Ned. I thought he was probably right.

The streets here weren't as empty as in other parts of the city, but most of the people we saw were poor.

"Yes, all the rich are long gone to the country – unless the plague got them first," said George.

"Have a little patience, lads," said Bad Barnaby. "We'll find a quiet corner where we can keep an eye out and wait. Someone will turn up."

He led us to a narrow alley down Cheapside, where we stood out of sight in the shadows. Bad Barnaby peered round the corner every so often, searching the street for a likely victim, talking to me in a low voice about what I had to do.

"Once we've got someone lined up, all you have to do is talk to him," he said. "Tell him the tragic story of how you were orphaned, tell him you know where he can buy an elixir that is guaranteed to keep him safe from the pestilence. In fact, tell him anything that will hold his attention while we sneak up on him. You can manage that, can't you? Then we get to work with our cudgels and relieve him of his money."

"What if I refuse?" I said.

"You won't, not if you know what's good for you," he growled. He grabbed hold of me by the front of my jacket and stared into my eyes. "Just remember, boy, we'll be hiding nearby and you can be sure we'll catch you. Then you'll be sorry. . ."

Once again, I had no choice. There were three of them, so it would be hard to get away. But how could I do what they were asking? It would mean I was tricking someone, and that almost seemed worse than actually stealing. My parents had always taught me it was wrong to lie or cheat, or to be involved in anything deceitful. Now I would have to do all of that just to protect myself.

"Pssst! Barnaby!" George said suddenly. "I think we've found our man."

Bad Barnaby let me go and turned to look out into the street. I did too and I soon saw the man George meant. He was clean-shaven and I guessed him to be in his mid-thirties or thereabouts. His jacket and breeches were of the finest quality, as were his shoes. He wore a white shirt with a lace collar and a fashionable, broad-brimmed hat with a peacock's feather stuck in the band. The gentleman carried a leather satchel as well, one rather like mine, if a bit bigger. I always carried mine with me in case there was ever an opportunity to escape. It contained nothing but my family's Bible, but I didn't want to have to go back for it if I ever managed to run away.

"He looks like a real prize," Bad Barnaby whispered happily. "Off you go then, boy," he hissed, his breath hot on my ear. "Don't fail me now – or else."

He shoved me hard in the back, pushing me out into the street and in front of the man. I stumbled but stayed on my feet and the man stopped, a puzzled frown on his face. I raised my eyes to his and for a moment we stared at each other. There was no one else nearby. I could no longer see Bad Barnaby or the other two, but I knew they were still there, creeping towards their victim. I opened my mouth to do as I had been told . . . but then I realized I did have a choice after all. I could help to trick this man and save myself from a beating, then he would be the one to suffer. Or I could warn him and have a clean conscience. Put like that it was no choice at all, really.

"Run!" I yelled, before I could change my mind. "Get away from here while you still can!"

He seemed startled and took a step backwards. I heard Bad Barnaby roaring curses and I looked round. He was emerging from the alley, cudgel at the ready, murder in his eyes. Ned and George were close behind him. The man clearly didn't need any more convincing. His eyes grew wide with fear and he spun around, running back the way he had come.

I sprinted after him – there was no other way for me to go. The man was surprisingly fast, spurred on by fear. I only just kept up with him and I expected to be grabbed from behind at any moment. But gradually the sound of thudding footsteps and heavy breathing began to fade, and I dared to look over my shoulder. We were well ahead and they were slowing down.

I looked round again. Old St Paul's was looming over us. Bad Barnaby clearly didn't want anybody to see him getting up to his dirty work and there were people in the streets around the cathedral. The gentleman seemed to grasp this as well and made a final dash to the steps. He stopped at the top. I joined him and we stood together, gasping for breath.

"They've given up, I think," the gentleman said at last. He nodded in the direction of our pursuers. They were walking away down Cheapside, trying to look casual. The man turned to me and smiled. "Thank you for saving me from those footpads, young man. What is your name? I am Samuel Burgess."

"My name?" I whispered. I had almost forgotten it while I had been Bad Barnaby's slave. He had called me "boy", and worse. But my true name was still there somewhere, hidden inside. I was still me, youngest son of John and Meg, brother to William and Henry. "My name is Daniel Page, sir," I said.

"It is a pleasure to meet you, Daniel Page," he said, holding out his hand.

I smiled at him and we shook hands.

Master Burgess asked if I would like to go to his house with him and have something to eat as thanks for stopping Bad Barnaby and his gang. I hesitated, reluctant to follow another stranger. He seemed like a good man, but how could I be sure? I had begun to lose my faith in people as well as God. Josiah had seemed good, but he had turned out to be evil. What if the same happened with this Master Burgess?

Bad Barnaby, however, had kept me hungry and thirsty, and my stomach was so empty it hurt. So I said yes and we set off. We didn't have far to go. Master Burgess had a fine house just beyond Cornhill, in Leadenhall Street. A maid opened the door to us when we arrived and Master Burgess sent her off to tell the cook that he had brought a guest for supper. Then another young woman appeared, but I could tell she was no servant. She had thick brown hair and green eyes, and she wore a fine dress of light-blue silk. I knew instantly she was the mistress of the house.

"Well, who have we here then?" she said, frowning as she looked me up and down. "Don't tell me – another one of your waifs and strays! I thought we had agreed—"

"Daniel, let me introduce you to Abigail, my dear wife," said Master Burgess. "And this, my love, is Daniel Page. I know what we agreed, but Daniel is a special case – he rescued me from a gang of footpads. I am sure he saved my life!"

"Did he, now?" said Mistress Burgess, raising a sceptical eyebrow. "And why did he do that? He looks like a thief himself. He smells like one, too."

She wrinkled her nose and I blushed. I realized that she was right. I had escaped from home with few clothes, just an extra undershirt and a change of drawers, and I had lost both a long time ago. My jacket and breeches were filthy and my shoes were scuffed. At home Mother had always insisted we bathe ourselves in a tub once a week, but I couldn't remember the last time I had washed. Now I felt ashamed to be standing in front of these rich people in such a terrible state.

I turned to leave, desperate to escape and find some dark corner where I could hide. But Master Burgess stood between me and the door and wouldn't let me go.

"Come, Abigail, we must feed the poor boy," he said. "I'd like to hear about his experiences, too – that might help me in my work."

"Oh, very well," his wife said with a sigh.

They gave me the best meal I had eaten in a long time, a dish of oysters and white fish, with fine white bread and some apples. Master Burgess asked me all sorts of questions. To begin with, I was careful about how I answered, not wanting to tell these strangers too much about myself. But soon I felt an urge to tell them everything that I had seen and done. The words started pouring from my mouth and I simply couldn't stop them.

CHAPTER

9

I don't know how long I talked for. We were sitting at an oak table in a large room, me on one side, Master and Mistress Burgess opposite. To begin with, Master Burgess kept interrupting me to ask questions and I briefly wondered what he had meant about my experiences helping him in his work. But after a while he fell silent and just listened, as did Mistress Burgess. Eventually I finished my story and pushed away my bowl.

"Thank you for the meal," I said, getting to my feet.

"I think I'd better go now." I felt that they had helped me enough and that I didn't want to outstay my welcome, even though I had no idea where I should go next.

"You will do no such thing," said Mistress Burgess, jumping up too. She dabbed at her eyes with a small handkerchief, moved by my story. "I have never heard such a sad tale! I cannot even imagine what your poor mother must have suffered. No, you will stay here and we will take care of you. Samuel, go and tell Reuben to prepare a bath. And we must find Daniel some new clothes. Tell Molly to go next door and ask Mistress Johnson if she has something…"

It turned out that Molly was the maid who had opened the door to us and Reuben was another servant. There was a cook called Jane, too. Reuben prepared a bath for me in the large scullery, heating a lot of water over the fire and pouring it into an iron tub. He left me on my own to get undressed, then came back to collect my clothes once I was in the bath. I lay in the water. It was wonderful to be clean again.

Reuben returned, with new clothes, borrowed

from Master Burgess's neighbours, who had a son my age and size. My old clothes and shoes had been burned, by order of Mistress Burgess. I felt a pang of sadness – they were a link to my mother, but as I had worn them for months, I knew they were beyond saving.

After I was dressed, Reuben took me back to the room with the oak table. Master and Mistress Burgess were still sitting there. They smiled when I came in.

"That's better," said Mistress Burgess. "You are completely transformed, Daniel."

"I think it is rather that he has returned to his true self," said Master Burgess.

They were both right, but I couldn't think of the words to explain how I felt. I burst into tears instead and sobbed even more when Mistress Burgess rose from her seat and hurried round the table to hold me.

Only my mother had held me like this before and she was gone forever.

Samuel and Abigail gave me a small room of my own in the attic, next to the room where Reuben slept. They insisted from the beginning that I use their

Christian names, which was strange to me at first. My parents had always taught me to be respectful to my elders and betters, and that should have meant calling them "Sir" and "My Lady", but I quickly got used to it and I realized it was typical of Samuel and Abigail. They had no airs and graces.

Samuel was a physician, a word I had heard before but never really understood. I discovered it meant he was someone who had studied medicine at Oxford University, so I thought that he was probably the kind of Oxford philosopher Josiah had often spoken of. But unlike Josiah, Samuel had not studied medicine so he could make money from the sick and suffering. Samuel wanted to help people and he visited the sick to do just that, offering them remedies he had devised himself. He also wanted to find out more about the plague.

"All things have origins, and that includes sicknesses," he said to me, after I had been living with them for a few days. He was showing me his study, a room that contained more jars of liquids and potions and powders and body parts than Josiah's. Samuel had far more books than Josiah as well.

"The pestilence must have a cause and I believe that one day we will know what it is. Then perhaps we will be able to find proper cures for this terrible illness."

It was fascinating to listen to someone who knew so much and who was so keen to do good. I worried about where God fitted into Samuel's theories, although I tried not to think about that. But Samuel didn't seem to have these doubts. His faith in God was as strong as that of my parents, despite the plague, and he believed that God had begun to reveal more of his creation – if you knew where to look.

"The times are changing, Daniel," Samuel said. He often talked of the Royal Society, a club that had been set up by men who wanted to find out more about the world. It was supported by King Charles, so Samuel had a great deal of respect for our monarch. The men of the Royal Society studied lots of things, and Samuel said they were beginning to make people think differently.

It had always been believed that our bodies contained four liquids, or "humours" – blood, yellow bile, black bile and phlegm. These had to be kept in balance or we would fall ill. One way to prevent that happening was to "bleed" people. That meant opening a vein and allowing some blood to drain out, which would restore the balance of the humours. Samuel told me that a member of the Royal Society – a clever man called Robert Boyle – thought that was nonsense. He believed instead that everything in the world was actually made up of tiny particles we couldn't see, and that tiny particles of the pestilence might find their way into our bodies and make us fall ill.

It made sense to me. After all, the pestilence often seemed to pass from person to person, especially if they touched each other or were cooped up together in a confined space. People had always suspected that was what happened, but without knowing how. This idea of particles was one way it could be explained, I thought. The plague particles might be passed on by a sick person's breath or through their sweat.

"So you don't think the plague is caused by a poisonous miasma, or that it's a punishment from God?" I asked Samuel. "But that's what a lot of people believe, isn't it?"

"I wouldn't dare to think that I know what God's plans are," Samuel said. "As for the theory of the miasma . . . well, that may have some merit, but it has always seemed strange to me that the pestilence starts in places where the poor live, and where there are lots of other diseases. Poverty and disease go together, Daniel, and sometimes I think we could cure disease if we cured poverty. It is also strange that some people, such as you and I, seem to be able to resist the illness. And then there are even those who seem doomed but survive. I have heard reports of several people who were left to die at the side of plague pits but then recovered."

I began to understand why Samuel had asked me so many questions about my experiences. This was the method pursued by Samuel and his friends – ask as many questions as possible and write down all the answers so you could see any hidden patterns that would lead to the causes of things being revealed. I found it all really fascinating and eventually I asked Samuel if I could help him with his work.

"I could carry your bag when you go to visit the sick,"

I suggested one evening. "I could even help you with your notes – I can read and write quite well."

"That is a generous offer, Daniel," he said. "But I do not think I can accept."

"What are you talking about, Samuel?" Abigail said crossly. She often sat with us and joined in with our conversations about Samuel's work. "I insist you do as Daniel asks. It will mean that you have someone sensible with you, someone who can make sure you come to no harm. Consider your offer accepted, Daniel."

I smiled to myself. Samuel and Abigail had not been married long. Abigail was much younger than her husband, perhaps only twenty, and she loved him deeply and was fiercely protective of him. She worried about him whenever he was out of the house, because she knew he went to dangerous places. He had also brought back other needy souls before me, the waifs and strays she had mentioned when I first arrived. Some had been less than honest, which explained why she had been so stern with him when he had brought me home. I was proud to know I was the first "waif" they had taken in.

"Don't worry, Abigail," I said. "I promise that I will look after him."

Now Abigail smiled and I knew I had said the right thing.

August turned into September and the hot weather broke at last. One morning in the middle of the month a cool wind swept in from the west, bringing rain in its skirts, and our stricken city seemed to sigh with relief. The plague began to abate as well – every day the number of the dead on the Bills of Mortality grew less and less.

But for me there was one more strange surprise to come.

CHAPTER

10

A mild, wet autumn turned into a cold winter and the plague finally slowed down. Samuel said that if Robert Boyle's theory was right, then perhaps the cold made the plague particles move more slowly than in the heat of the summer. Other people simply said that God had heard our prayers at last and had decided to show us his love and mercy.

Whatever the reason, things slowly began to return to normal in the city. In the new year – the year of our Lord 1666 – the dead carts were no longer seen in the streets and the plague pits were filled with quicklime to speed up the decay of the bodies, then covered with a thick layer of soil. Some people still fell ill, but there were fewer with each passing week and they were no longer locked in their houses.

Those who had fled gradually began to return, leaving behind their makeshift camps on the edge of the city. The poor came back first, because they often had nowhere else to go, although many families were scattered across the counties around London. Then came the middling sort, eager to get their businesses reopened. The rich came back in the spring, including King Charles and his family. Soon the streets were lively again and a visitor who had never seen London before might have been forgiven for thinking that the plague had not been so bad after all.

I knew differently, however. There were too many empty houses, and wherever I looked the streets seemed full of ghosts. The shadow of the plague still hung over those of us who had survived. The laughter I heard was brittle and forced, and I saw many more sad faces than happy ones. Samuel said the pestilence had been a terrible disaster – over 100,000 people had died in London, around one person in every four who had lived in the city.

The rule of law returned to the city with the king. He and the Lord Mayor put soldiers on the streets, and before long many rogues were brought to justice. For a while the courts were kept busy. So were the executioners at Tyburn to the west of the city, the crossroads where those who broke the law had always been hanged. That's where Bad Barnaby ended his days, anyway, along with Ned and George. Samuel told me they had been caught while trying to rob a man and condemned to death. They were hanged together on a blustery day in March. I was not sorry to hear of their fate, even though I knew it would have been more Christian to forgive them for what they had done to me. Abigail told me not to be so hard on myself when I admitted how I felt.

"They treated you cruelly, Daniel," she said. "God knows that, and he will look into your heart and forgive *you* for how you feel."

Not long after that I discovered what had happened to Josiah. I was out with Samuel one day, accompanying him on a visit to a sick family, when I realized we were walking along Blowbladder Street. I paused to glance down the familiar alley. A bright red cross had been painted on Josiah's door, along with the usual words, *Lord Have Mercy Upon Us*. It seemed that the plague had caught up with this Doctor Beak after all.

Soon spring turned into another hot, dry summer. Samuel and Abigail made it clear they were happy for me to stay with them for as long as I liked. Samuel even talked of taking me on as his apprentice. I loved learning from him, it was as if a whole new life was opening up before me, one in which I could do something truly worthwhile. I thought that Mother and Father would have been proud to see how well I was progressing.

The horrors I had seen and experienced had faded in my mind too. Why then did I feel so restless? I fell back into my old habit of roaming the streets, almost as if I were searching for something. Then one day I realized it was not something, but someone – I had no proof that Mother had died, and a tiny part of me had never given up hope she might still be alive and that we would be reunited. Whenever I glimpsed a woman of the same age or height, my heart would start hammering, but it was never her. One time, I was sure I heard a voice that sounded exactly like hers in the next street, but when I ran round the corner, nobody was there.

Then the Great Fire came, and seemed to burn away the past entirely.

The fire started that September in a baker's shop in Pudding Lane, then spread to most of the city. Only those of us who were there during the four nights and three days of the fire know what it was like – the roaring flames and choking smoke, the hellish heat, the sheer terror and panic among the people of a city that had already suffered so much.

Once more, the roads out of the city were choked with carts and coaches and those fleeing on foot. For a while it seemed the flames would burn on until they destroyed the whole of England, swept on by an east wind. But at last they began to recede. Some said it was because the wind dropped, others because the king's soldiers used gunpowder to blow up rows of buildings and create firebreaks to stop it spreading.

Most people didn't care why it had stopped and were just glad it was over.

We were lucky in Leadenhall Street. The fire came close enough for the roof to get a little singed, but that was all. Samuel worked long hours helping those who had been burned or made ill by the smoke and Abigail took in many of their friends who had been made homeless. I did whatever I could, going out with Samuel to be his assistant and helping the servants around the house.

It wasn't until a week after the fire stopped that things seemed to calm down. One morning I felt that old restlessness again and I set off to roam the streets. I was also curious to see what the flames had done to my city. The answer was shocking – I found almost nothing but ruins wherever I went, nearly every street burned to the ground, the buildings reduced to ashes, the air still reeking of fire and smoke.

I walked up Cheapside and stood in front of old St Paul's, or rather what was left of it. The central tower was standing, but the great roof had gone and the walls were black where the flames had licked at them. The inside was burned out and it looked as if the building might collapse any minute. Samuel had said people were already arguing about whether it should be saved or replaced by a completely new cathedral.

I turned away and walked towards Bear Alley, heading back to where I began my journey over a year before. The fire had burned very fiercely here – to begin with I could not even find where Bread Street began. I worked it out eventually and walked along it to Bear Alley. At last I came to the ruin of my home.

It had been almost entirely destroyed – only a part of one wall remained. Oddly enough, it was the wall with the window I had climbed out of that night, although that was now merely a scorched frame. I peered through it, as if I would be able to see into the past, to my home as it once was.

Mother's pale face stared back at me.

I closed my eyes and shook my head. My mind was playing tricks on me, conjuring up her face in the window, as it had been the last time I'd seen her. I opened my eyes and she had gone. Then someone spoke behind me.

"Daniel, is that really you?"

I slowly turned round. It was Mother. She had

come out of the ashes of our house and stood with one hand stretched out towards me. She wore a long black dress and a small cloak around her shoulders. Her neck was no longer swollen with the tokens of the sickness.

"Yes, it's me," I said, unable to take my eyes off her. "Are you a ghost?"

It was the only possible explanation. Mother had died and gone to Heaven, and God had allowed her to return to Earth to visit me.

"No, Daniel," she said, smiling. "Touch my hand and I'll prove it to you."

I reached out, our fingertips met and then she grasped my hand and pulled me towards her. I don't know how long we held on to each other.

"But I came back to the house the day after I escaped and you weren't here," I said. "I was sure you were dead. What happened? How did you survive?"

"I don't remember much," she said. "I saw the watchman chasing you, but I must have fainted. I thought I would wake in Heaven, but my next memory is of Hell. Or at least, of something a lot like it.

I was in a dead cart and being taken to a pit to be buried. Then they saw that I was alive and they left me by the side of the pit. A kindly priest found me and cared for me. He took me to a refuge."

Mother told me how she had recovered slowly and had stayed with several different families – friends of the priest who had first found her. When she was strong enough she had returned to London to search for me, convinced I must still be alive. I wondered how many times we had walked along the same streets and just missed each other. But none of that mattered any more. We were together again.

I led Mother through the streets towards my new home, where I knew she would be welcome. My mind was racing. I had so much to tell her and so many questions to ask her. I had lots of plans too – I wondered if Mother could assist Abigail as I assisted Samuel. Perhaps they might even help her to find work as a seamstress again. But I knew one thing above all. For the time being at least I would take care of Mother as she had always taken care of me. I owed that much to her, and to Father and my brothers –

they would have wanted me to look after her as well as I could.

Somehow, I had survived the Great Plague and found my mother again. I prayed that we might both live ordinary, happy lives from this day forward.

I had a feeling that we would.

HISTORICAL NOTE:

THE GREAT PLAGUE

THE CITY OF LONDON

In 1665 London was much smaller than it is now, but it was still the biggest city in England and the third biggest city in Europe after Paris and Rome. It had a population of at least 400,000. Most of the city's buildings were still within the old Roman walls and north of the River Thames. The king's palace at Whitehall was separate from the rest of London, and so was Westminster, where Parliament met in the shadow of the great abbey.

There were some large buildings in London – great

churches such as old St Paul's Cathedral and the houses of rich families. But most of the streets were very narrow and the houses were small. They were built mostly of wood and had thatched roofs. There were no sewers and the streets were full of rubbish and waste. So it's no surprise that there were rats everywhere.

The seventeenth century was a difficult time for the people of London. The Civil War (1642–1651) between King Charles I and Parliament had been brutal, and the country was still politically divided. Then there was the outbreak of the Great Plague in 1665, which was followed by the Great Fire of 1666. The fire destroyed most of the city, including the great cathedral of Saint Paul's, which was hundreds of years old. After a lot of debate, it was decided that London deserved a new cathedral with a beautiful dome. It was designed by the great architect Sir Christopher Wren, who played a major part in rebuilding the city. His cathedral still stands on Ludgate Hill to this day.

THE PLAGUE

Disease was a major cause of death in the seventeenth century. Medicine wasn't very advanced, and doctors knew little about what caused most illnesses or how to effectively treat them. The plague had been around for a long time and there were many theories about what caused it, most of them wrong. We now know that it's caused by a bacterium called *Yersinia pestis*, which is found in certain kinds of fleas. These fleas infected many of the rats in London and spread the sickness when they bit other creatures, including humans. When the Lord Mayor ordered all the cats in London to be killed, he took away one of the only things that kept the rats in check. More rats meant more fleas to infect people, who would then infect each other – especially if they were locked into houses together. There had been an outbreak of the plague in the Netherlands in the early 1660s, and some historians believe that infected rats from a Dutch ship brought the disease to London in early 1665.

It's hard to know exactly how many people died in the outbreak. The Bills of Mortality that Daniel saw pasted up were quite good at listing the numbers of the dead, but it's difficult to work out how many of them were actually caused by the plague. People often didn't want to admit that members of their family had died of the plague, so may have listed the cause of death as something else. But modern historians think that at least 100,000 people died of the plague, and perhaps more. The plague still exists today, but advances in medicine and improvements in living conditions mean that it is no longer such a terrible threat.

THE PEOPLE

Most of the people in this story are fictional, including Daniel and his family, but their experiences are based on historical accounts of people who lived during the seventeenth century. Most Londoners were Protestant Christians, like Daniel's parents, and there were also strict Protestants called Puritans who wanted to live a plain and simple life. During the plague, the authorities did appoint men like Bad Barnaby to be watchmen, and many of them took bribes from the people they were supposed to be keeping locked up and let them out – or broke in and looted their houses.

There were also plenty of "plague doctors", many of whom dressed as Doctor Beak and sold fake medicines to desperate people, like Josiah in the story. They were sometimes called "quack doctors" or just "quacks" because people said they talked so much when they were trying to sell their potions that they sounded like a flock of ducks quacking. But there were men like Samuel too, physicians who were increasingly trying to find out the real causes of diseases and work out ways to treat them successfully. It was the beginning of modern science – people were starting to question many things, including religion, and were attempting to build an understanding of the natural world around them. To this end, the Royal Society was founded in 1660, an organization that supported scientific thinking. Sir Christopher Wren was a member, as were many of the greatest thinkers of the time, including Sir Isaac Newton.

King Charles I and his son King Charles II were real historical figures, as was the Lord Protector, Oliver Cromwell. Charles II died in 1685 and was followed onto the throne by his younger brother, James II. But James was even less popular than his father and brother, and was deposed in 1688. Parliament reasserted its power, and ever since then the king or queen has had had less political influence.

HISTORICAL ACCOUNTS

The Great Plague was one of the worst disasters ever to strike London, so a lot was written about it at the time. Records such as the Bills of Mortality have been very useful to historians in building up a picture of how the plague developed and what happened. But there were plenty of personal records, too. Samuel Pepys was a man who worked for the government and he wrote a great deal about the plague in his famous diaries. Daniel Defoe, the author of *Robinson Crusoe*, a novel about a man shipwrecked on an island, was only a child during the Great Plague, but years later he wrote a book called *A Journal of the Plague Year,* which tells us a lot about what happened in 1665. In this story, the character Samuel Burgess is partly based on a real physician of the time called Nathaniel Hodges, who also wrote about the plague in his journals.

TIMELINE

1534 King Henry VIII breaks with the Roman Catholic Church.

1558 Henry VIII's daughter becomes Queen Elizabeth I.

1603 Elizabeth I dies and is succeeded by a distant cousin, James VI of Scotland, who becomes James I of England.

1605 The Gunpowder Plot. Guy Fawkes attempts to blow up Parliament and James I. He fails and is executed.

1625 James's son Charles I becomes king.

1633 Samuel Pepys (1633–1703) the famous diarist is born.

1642 The Civil War begins. Oliver Cromwell forms the New Model Army. Charles I is defeated.

1649 Charles I is tried and beheaded and the Commonwealth is set up

1653 Oliver Cromwell becomes Lord Protector of England.

1658 Oliver Cromwell dies.

1660 The monarchy is restored. Charles I's son Charles II becomes king.

1665 The year of the Great Plague in London.

1666 The Great Fire of London (2nd–5th September)

IF YOU ENJOYED

PLAGUE

OUTBREAK IN LONDON, 1665–1666

READ ON FOR A TASTE OF

INDEPENDENCE

WAR IN IRELAND, 20–21 NOVEMBER 1920

PROLOGUE

21 NOVEMBER 1920
CROKE PARK, DUBLIN

We made our way in through the turnstiles, and headed for Hill 60, a grassy hill that had been built at the railway end of Croke Park to give spectators a chance to get a better view. We found ourselves a spot about halfway up the hill.

More and more spectators poured in through the turnstiles, climbing the hill and filling up the terraces. By the time the match was ready to begin, it looked like there were at least five thousand people inside Croke Park. A huge crowd.

After the usual announcements and introductions, the two teams came out onto the pitch to be met with a huge roar – the Dubs in their sky-blue shirts and Tipp in their white jerseys with a green diagonal sash.

"Dubs! Dubs!" and "Jackeens!" we shouted, which were the Dublin rallying cries. The Tipperary supporters responded with a chorus of, "Tipp! Tipp!"

For the first time since meeting Michael Collins and the other IRA members, I was able to think about something other than what I'd heard. I stopped thinking about anything other than the match. This was going to be a clash of giants, the two best football teams in Ireland!

The game started brilliantly, the players showing their skills as they kicked, caught and passed at a speed that made your heart stop. The game had only been going on for a few minutes when we heard a shot ring out. The sound of it cut through the noise of the crowd and everyone fell silent.

The players stopped, bewildered and unsure of what was happening. Then suddenly we saw a force of Tans rush in from the turnstiles end, rifles levelled, firing into the crowd and at the players.

There was panic. The crowd yelling and rushing to try and get away.

"Make for the wall!" shouted Sean, pointing to the wall that bordered the canal end. I could see that the people nearest to the wall were already climbing it to get out, but as they reached the top we heard gunfire from outside the stadium and they fell back down. They were being shot at!

"The Tans are outside, on the canal bridge!" shouted Con. "There's no way out that way!"

Bullets were thudding around us.

"Get down!" shouted Sean. He grabbed me and threw me on the ground. "Crawl towards the main gate!"

I started to crawl. As I did, I glanced towards the pitch. Some of the players had managed to run towards the terraces, but others were lying on the grass. Some moved, some didn't. Con and Rory were crawling alongside us. Con got to his feet.

"For goodness sake, there are women and children here!" he shouted at the Tans.

The next second, I saw him stumble back and then fall. Blood was spreading out over his white shirt from beneath his jacket.

"Da!" screamed Rory.

Uncle Sean dived for his brother, getting to Con just before Rory.

"He's alive," Sean shouted at Rory. "He's just wounded."

He looked pretty badly wounded to me. He was unconscious, his eyes closed and his mouth open. His face was deathly white.

"Liam, get Rory to safety," said Sean. "I'll look after Con."

"But—" I began, feeling helpless. "I don't know what to do!"

"Just go!" shouted Sean. "Keep Rory with you. Make for home. I'll see you back there."

Rory was crying, his body heaving with great sobs as he looked at his father lying on the ground.

"Come on, Rory," I said. I took him by the arm, but he shook me off.

"I'm staying with my da!" he burst out.

"No, you're not," Sean shouted at him. "Your da will be all right. Go! Go with Liam and do what he tells you. Go now!"

CHAPTER

1

"Pay attention, Liam! You'll drop that bag if you're not careful, and there's eggs in it!"

"Sorry, Aunt Mary," I said.

I was supposed to be helping my aunt carry the shopping, but all I could think of was the big match the next day. Tomorrow, Sunday, was the day of the Gaelic Athletic Association, the GAA, football final between Dublin and Tipperary at Croke Park. I couldn't wait because I had tickets for it, along with my uncles Sean and Con, and Con's son, my younger cousin, Rory.

My name's Liam Donnelly. I'm eleven years old and I live in Kilmainham in Dublin with my Uncle Sean and my Aunt Mary. On Saturday mornings Aunt Mary ropes me into helping her with the shopping, which means I end up carrying the heaviest bags. I don't mind because Aunt Mary lets me choose a sweet from McGinty's Toffee Shop as payment, so it's a fair deal.

My da, Patrick Donnelly, was killed in the Easter Rising of 1916, and my ma, Katharine, died in the flu epidemic of 1918 that followed the Great War. Uncle Sean and Aunt Mary's own daughters, my little cousins Maeve and Nuala, died during the same flu epidemic. They were just three years old. Over fifty million people around the world died in that flu epidemic of 1918, a quarter of a million in Ireland and Britain alone, but the death of my ma was what I remembered. Uncle Sean and Aunt Mary kept a shrine to Maeve and Nuala in their bedroom. I kept a shrine for my ma in my heart.

It was after my ma and my little cousins died that Uncle Sean and Aunt Mary took me in and gave me a home. They've been as good as any parent could ever be to me, but I still think about my poor ma and da and wonder what life would be like for me if they hadn't died.

Anyway, this Saturday morning we'd nearly finished our shopping. We were just coming out of Derry's, the butchers, when we were stopped by two Tans, who pointed their rifles at us.

"What you got in your bag?" demanded one with a scowl.

Black and Tans was the name we'd given to the thugs from England who'd been sent to join with the men of the Royal Irish Constabulary (RIC). The first Tans arrived in Ireland just last year, when the British realized they were losing the war against the Irish Republican Army (IRA) and they needed more men. Most of these thugs had been soldiers in the British army during the Great War, though some were men who'd been let out of British jails if they signed up to join the Tans. They still act like they're soldiers or criminals, even though they're supposed to be part of the RIC.

They're known as the Black and Tans because of the uniforms they wear. The RIC didn't have enough proper uniforms for them when they first arrived, so they wear British army khaki trousers and RIC bottle-green tunics, which are almost black, although Uncle Sean says the "Black" comes from the colour of their hearts, because they are the nastiest and most violent creatures who ever walked God's earth.

When our war started in 1919, it was Irishmen fighting for freedom from British rule. Irish volunteers in everyday clothes, using whatever weapons they could find, often old rifles that had been used to shoot rabbits on farms. On the British side was the Royal Irish Constabulary; mostly Irishmen themselves, but paid by the British Government, who believed that Ireland should still be part of the British Empire. Backing the RIC was the British army – one of the most powerful armies in the world. The British army had just won a war against Germany. The Irish volunteers wanted us to have the freedom to rule ourselves. They wanted a government of Irish people, voted for by Irish people, to make the decisions on how Ireland should be run, instead of all the decisions being made in the British Parliament in London.

My Uncle Sean says the British thought that, with

their better weapons and their military training, they could put down the Irish volunteers quickly, just as they had in the uprising of 1916 when my da was killed.

But the Irish volunteers weren't put down. Instead they got better organized and became an actual army – the Irish Republican Army. In the countryside, they ambushed the British soldiers and the RIC, then stole away. In the towns and cities, they shot at the British soldiers and then vanished into the streets. Their success was mostly thanks to Michael Collins. He's the military commander of the IRA. Collins is a genius and a hero. He's always coming up with ways to defeat the British by any means. One of his best tactics is arming small groups with pistols and directing them to make surprise attacks and escape quickly before the enemy can go after them. The IRA are our own people; they know the country and the streets of where we live like the backs of their hands, so they can disappear fast.

Because the British think that Michael Collins is so dangerous, they're offering a reward of ten thousand pounds to anyone who can capture him, dead or alive. Ten thousand pounds! That's more money than most people will see in their lifetime! Or in lots of lifetimes around here. But the Irish people are loyal to Collins and no one has ever even thought of betraying him. My Uncle Sean says freedom is worth more than any amount of money. And if anyone did betray Michael Collins, that traitor would be killed before he was able to collect the reward.

Most Irish people would rather get into real trouble with the Black and Tans than hand in one of our own. Of all the British forces fighting us, soldiers and police, the Black and Tans are the worst. Everyone I know thinks they are evil and get their fun from bullying women and children. Like they were doing now, with Aunt Mary and me.

When Aunt Mary didn't answer, just glared back at them, the Tan repeated his question in a nastier tone of voice.

"I said: what you got in your bag?" he growled.

"Shopping," replied Aunt Mary, looking at the pair of them coldly.

"Open it!" he snarled, and he poked the end of his rifle hard into Aunt Mary's shopping bag, making her stumble backwards.

"Leave her alone!" I shouted at him.

The other one swung his free hand, hitting me round the head with such a clout that I saw stars and tears came to my eyes.

"He's lying!" snarled the one who'd hit me. "Shoot the boy!"

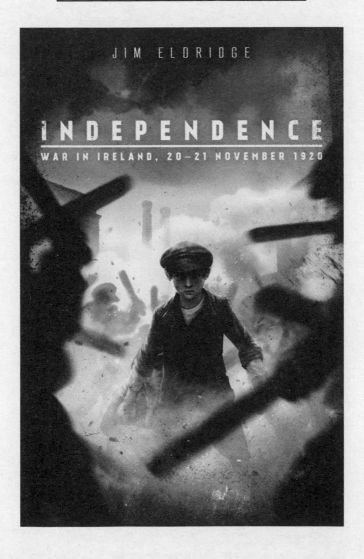

JIM ELDRIDGE

INDEPENDENCE

WAR IN IRELAND, 20–21 NOVEMBER 1920